The Climb

JOHN ESCOTT

Level 3

Series Editors: Andy Hopkins and Jocelyn Potter

Pearson Education Limited
Edinburgh Gate, Harlow,
Essex CM20 2JE, England
and Associated Companies throughout the world.

ISBN: 978-1-4058-8179-1

First published 2000
This edition first published 2008

6

Copyright © Pearson Education Ltd 2008
Illustrations by Jon Sayer

Typeset by Graphicraft Ltd, Hong Kong
Set in 11/14pt Bembo
Printed in China
SWTC/06

Published by Pearson Education Ltd

Every effort has been made to trace the copyright holders and we apologise in advance
for any unintentional omissions. We would be pleased to insert the appropriate
acknowledgement in any subsequent edition of this publication.

For a complete list of the titles available in the Pearson English Readers series, please visit
www.pearsonenglishreaders.com. Alternatively, write to your local Pearson Education
office or to Pearson English Readers Marketing Department, Pearson Education,
Edinburgh Gate, Harlow, Essex CM20 2JE, England.

Contents

Introduction

'What's the matter?' Eleni asked Costas when they were inside the house. 'You look worried. Is something wrong?'

'I'm sure I've seen Mr Holland before,' Costas said.

'But where?' Eleni said. 'He says he's never been to the island.'

'I know he said that,' Costas said. 'But I don't believe him.'

Who is the stranger who has come to the little island off the coast of Greece? Why is he here? Why does he look at Eagle's Rock, and at Mr Vitalis's house? What is the mystery about this man who calls himself 'Holland'? Is that his real name? What is his secret? Mr Vitalis is the richest man on the island. Does he have a secret, too? And have the two men met before?

Costas and his sister, Eleni, want to know the answers to these questions. And Costas also wants to climb the dangerous Eagle's Rock. People have died while trying to climb it. But Costas loves climbing, and he is not afraid.

'I want to be the first person to climb it to the top,' he says. 'Then I'll be famous.'

'Or dead,' says Eleni.

John Escott writes books for students of all ages. Most of all he likes writing mystery and detective stories. He lives in Bournemouth, a large town on the south coast of England. When he isn't writing, he enjoys long walks by the sea, along empty beaches. He also likes looking for forgotten books in little back-street bookshops.

John's other books written for Pearson English Readers include *The Missing Coins* and *Lost in New York*.

Chapter 1   A Man Called Holland

It began one day in the summer. It was the day that the man came to the island. The man who called himself Holland.

It was early in the morning. The plane flew in a circle above the island, and then it began to come down. Holland was nervous. He looked out of the window at the island below. It was beautiful, but he thought to himself, 'Was I right to come?'

The plane landed just as the sun came up. Holland walked across to the airport building with the other passengers. It was already hot.

He was travelling alone. It was his first visit and it was probably his last. A second visit was probably too dangerous.

'I don't have to do it,' he thought. 'There's still time to say no. I can get on the next plane and fly out of here, away from this island.'

But he knew that this wasn't really possible. He needed the money. He needed it badly.

He saw a telephone and walked across to it. He took a notebook from his pocket. Then he turned the pages until he found a number. His hand was shaking as he picked up the phone.

'Hello?' said a voice at the other end.

Holland knew the voice. 'It's me,' he said. 'I've arrived.'

'Ah, good,' the voice said. 'Your flight is on time.'

'Where am I staying?' Holland asked.

'In a holiday villa on the cliff,' the voice said.

'OK,' Holland said.

'You sound nervous. You *are* going to do the job, aren't you?'

'I don't know,' Holland said. 'I told you before. I want to see the place first. I want to see exactly what I have to do.'

'You'll be able to see the house from the villa,' said the voice at the other end. 'That's what you wanted?'

'Yes,' Holland said. 'But how do I get there?'

'Pick up a car and a map from the airport garage. They're both waiting for you, in the name of Holland. You'll find the villa easily. It's on the cliff road. It belongs to a man called Kazakou. He knows nothing, of course.'

'What about the money?' Holland asked.

'You'll get it later today,' the voice said. 'Half the money now. The other half after the job's done.'

'Where do I meet–?'

'I've already told you that!' The voice sounded angry now.

'Tell me again,' Holland said.

The voice told him.

'OK,' Holland said. 'Eleven o'clock. I'll be there.'

He put down the phone and went to the airport garage. The airport was half-empty. He looked at the faces of the other people. They were tourists on holiday, with none of the worries that he had. 'Will anybody know my face? I hope not,' thought Holland.

'I don't have to stay,' he thought. 'I can leave now.'

But he went to get the car.

♦

The island wasn't far from the coast of Greece. It was popular with people who wanted a quiet holiday. There weren't many bars, and there were no nightclubs. It was a place for people who liked to walk. Or they could swim, or sit in the small cafés with a glass of wine.

On another part of the island, a young man was climbing a cliff. His sister, Eleni, was swimming in the sea. Costas and his sister lived on the island. Their father, Mr Kazakou, owned a holiday villa and some holiday flats.

Costas was studying at university. He wanted to be a doctor. Eleni was still at school. But now they were home, on holiday. Eleni liked swimming. Costas liked climbing the cliffs around the island. The cliffs were high on this part of the island. They were shaped like a letter 'C' around the beach.

The beach was almost empty because it was still early in the morning. There were only a few people walking along the sand. Two or three others sat or stood outside their holiday flats. The island woke up slowly.

Costas liked to get up early and climb the rocks above the beach. That morning, Eleni decided to go with him. She wanted to have an early swim.

She was lying on her back in the water, looking up at the cliff. She looked around the cliff until she saw the small, brightly-coloured shape of her brother in his climbing clothes. He was half-way up the cliff.

'He's a better climber than he was,' she thought. 'But he gets into dangerous places. I don't like it when he climbs alone. It's more dangerous. I'm almost afraid to watch him.'

Some time later, Eleni looked across to the holiday villa that her father owned. It stood between other villas at one end of the cliff top.

There was a car outside Mr Kazakou's villa. It looked small from the sea. But Eleni could see that it was a long, low car with an open top. It wasn't a car that she knew.

'That car wasn't there earlier,' Eleni said to herself. 'It probably belongs to the person who's staying in the villa this week.'

She swam for another half hour. The water was warm and pleasant. She watched Costas make the climb back down. He began to walk towards the other end of the beach. The cliff was steeper there, and the rocks were more dangerous.

Eleni saw where he was going. She looked worried as she came out of the water.

Chapter 2   Eagle's Rock

Costas walked along the beach and looked up at the cliff at the end. The rocks were steep. One was shaped like the head of a bird; a large eagle with a sharp-looking beak.

There were signs at the bottom of the cliff.

DANGEROUS. KEEP AWAY. NO CLIMBING.

This rock was called Eagle's Rock. It was steep and dangerous to climb. Costas stood and looked up at it for a long time. He often thought about the rock. He even dreamed about it.

He thought about climbing it. But how? Which way? It was what he wanted to do. He dreamed of climbing Eagle's Rock almost every day now.

At the top of the cliff was a large white house with a long

garden down to the cliff edge. It was a very handsome house which belonged to a man called Mr Vitalis. He sometimes had guests, but he lived in the house alone for most of the time. He owned a computer company on the island. Almost everybody on the island knew him.

And everybody knew about Mr Vitalis' house. It was the biggest house on the island, and it had a high electric fence around three sides of the garden. The fence had a special burglar alarm. When somebody climbed over the fence, the alarm rang in the police station. Mr Vitalis wanted everybody to know that, too.

'I don't want burglars,' he said. 'So I tell everybody about my burglar alarm.'

There was no fence on the cliff side of the garden. There was no need for one. A person had to climb Eagle's Rock to get into the house on that side.

'And nobody's going to try that!' Mr Vitalis always said.

The house was called Eagle House, named after the cliff below it. It was a good name for a fine house.

But Costas wasn't looking at Mr Vitalis' house. He was looking at Eagle's Rock, thinking about the climb...

'Twenty-five metres high...follow the crack to the bird-shaped overhang. Move on slowly until it gets easier...then up the shelf above. Then a difficult climb for the next few metres...' he said to himself.

He was excited, just thinking about it.

Eleni dried herself with a towel and walked across the beach to Costas. She knew immediately what he was thinking about. She could see it in the look on his face. It worried her.

'Stop looking at it, Costas,' she said. 'Stop thinking about it. You can't climb Eagle's Rock – it's too dangerous. Two men and a woman have already died.'

That was true, Costas knew. There were a lot of accidents – and three deaths already – while people tried to climb the Rock.

'But don't you understand?' Costas said. 'I want to be the first person to climb it to the top. Then I'll be famous!'

'Or dead,' Eleni said.

Costas just laughed.

'Why don't you go up with other climbers, Costas?' Eleni said. 'It's much more dangerous to climb alone all the time. You frighten me.'

'You don't understand,' Costas said. 'It's more exciting. Just me against the cliff! A real test of my climbing skills – of my nerve!' His eyes shone as he spoke.

She took his arm and tried to pull him away from the cliff. She was angry with him now. 'Come home,' she said. 'I want a shower and some breakfast before I go to the shop.'

She pulled him away. 'All right,' Costas said at last.

'And don't tell father that you want to climb Eagle's Rock,' Eleni told him. 'He'll go crazy.'

Mr Kazakou didn't like his son climbing rocks and cliffs. He thought it was stupid. But Costas loved to climb. It excited him. It tested his nerve.

'I feel free!' he said. 'Just me and the birds. Sometimes I even feel like a bird up there!'

He tried to tell his father how he felt. But Mr Kazakou didn't listen. He didn't understand the excitement of using a climber's skill.

Eleni and her brother walked across the sand to the cliffs on the other side. They found the steps up to the cliff road above. The sun was warm on their backs.

'It's going to be a hot day today,' Eleni said.

The holiday villas were on the cliff road. Their father was outside the villa that he owned. He was a small man with a thick moustache and a happy smile.

'Costas! Eleni!' Mr Kazakou called to them. 'Come and meet Mr Holland.'

A fair-haired man stood next to Mr Kazakou. He didn't seem interested in meeting Costas or Eleni, but he waited. He watched them closely as they walked across to the garden of the villa. Costas and Eleni shook hands with him. Costas looked hard at the man's face until the man looked away.

'Mr Holland seems nervous,' Eleni thought.

'Mr Holland has come from England,' Mr Kazakou said. 'He's staying at the villa for two weeks. He's a writer.'

'A writer?' Eleni said. 'That's exciting! Do you write books?'

'Sometimes,' said the man. He didn't seem to want to talk about it.

'Have you been to the island before?' Costas asked him.

The man shook his head. 'No, never,' he said.

'I thought I knew your face,' Costas said.

'Do you have any friends on the island, Mr Holland?' Mr Kazakou asked.

Holland shook his head again. 'No. I know nobody on the island,' he said.

'There are a lot of good walks,' Mr Kazakou told him.

'Yes,' Holland said. 'Perhaps I'll do some walking.' Then he turned and went inside the villa.

Mr Kazakou walked back along the cliff road with Costas and Eleni. Their home was up the hill, in the town.

'Mr Holland didn't want to talk,' Costas said. 'He just wanted to get inside the villa.'

'Perhaps he's shy,' Mr Kazakou said. He was pleased that the man was staying at the villa for two weeks. It wasn't a good summer for tourists. 'Perhaps he just likes being alone.'

They walked up the hill to the small town. A few shops were open. A waiter was putting chairs and tables outside a small café. A woman was washing the step outside her house.

Costas was silent as he walked. 'Where have I seen Mr Holland before?' he thought. 'I'm sure I've seen him.'

Mr Kazakou went to help his wife in the garden. She was picking tomatoes for lunch.

'What's the matter?' Eleni asked Costas when they were inside the house. 'You look worried. Is something wrong?'

'I'm sure I've seen Mr Holland before,' Costas said.

'But where?' Eleni said. 'He says he's never been to the island.'

'I know he said that,' Costas said. 'But I don't believe him.'

Chapter 3   The Visit to the Shop

'Are you going out again?' Eleni asked her brother.

'Later,' Costas told her. 'First I have work to do. I have to finish a book and then write some notes.'

'Don't say anything to Father about Eagle's Rock,' she told him.

'He'll have to know soon,' Costas said. 'But I won't say anything yet.'

Eleni went to have a shower. Costas went up to his room to change his clothes.

Eleni dressed and ate some breakfast after her shower. Then she went off to the shop where she worked in the school holidays. The shop belonged to Mr Papas. It sold books and postcards. It also sold pictures from a small gallery at the back of the shop. Most of the pictures were by painters who lived on the island. Many tourists came into the shop, and to look at the paintings in the gallery.

'Good morning, Eleni,' Mr Papas said. 'I saw you swimming this morning. I waved, but you didn't see me.'

'Oh, I'm sorry, Mr Papas,' Eleni said. 'But it was lovely in the water.'

Mr Papas went for a long walk along the cliff each morning. 'I see that you have a visitor staying in your holiday villa,' he said. 'I saw an open-topped car outside in the road.'

'Yes,' Eleni said. And she told Mr Papas about Mr Holland. 'He's a writer.'

'Is he?' Mr Papas said. 'I'd like to meet him. I've never met a writer.'

'Perhaps he'll come to the shop and buy a book,' Eleni said.

She didn't say anything about Mr Holland's unfriendliness. Perhaps her father was right. Perhaps Mr Holland was just shy.

It was a quiet morning in the shop. There weren't many tourists that day. Eleni put some things in the window and tidied the bookshelves. Mr Papas went into the gallery to look at some new paintings.

Later, a large black car stopped outside, and a man got out. He was a big man and he wore a white suit.

'Mr Vitalis!' said Mr Papas, when the man came into the shop. 'It's good to see you again!'

Mr Vitalis liked buying paintings. Many of the paintings in his home – Eagle House – were by famous artists. Eleni knew about them from Mr Papas.

'The pictures are worth a lot of money,' she told Costas. 'Some are probably worth thousands and thousands of pounds. Mr Vitalis is very rich. He can buy as many paintings as he likes.'

Mr Vitalis came to the shop two or three times a year to see the new pictures. Sometimes he bought one. Mr Papas was always pleased to see the big man.

'Good morning, Mr Papas,' said Mr Vitalis. 'What can you show me today? Any interesting new paintings?'

'Good morning, Mr Vitalis,' Mr Papas said. He took the big man through to the gallery at the back of the shop. 'Make some coffee for Mr Vitalis, will you, Eleni?' he called over his shoulder.

Eleni went into the little kitchen at the side of the shop. She began to make some coffee.

The shop looked out onto the narrow road and a café opposite. A waiter stood in the doorway of the café, looking bored. There weren't many customers. There was a man sitting at one of the outside tables. He was drinking coffee and reading.

'It's Mr Holland!' Eleni said to herself.

'Eleni!' Mr Papas called from the gallery. 'Where's the coffee?'

'Coming, Mr Papas!' Eleni said.

She took the coffee into the gallery.

Mr Vitalis was looking at a picture. He seemed to like it. Mr Papas was watching him nervously. He was hoping to make a sale.

A woman came into the shop.

'Good morning,' Eleni said, going back into the shop.

The woman bought some postcards, and Eleni put them in a bag and took the money. Then a young man came in and bought a book.

Soon after that, Mr Vitalis and Mr Papas came out of the gallery. Mr Vitalis didn't want to buy any of the paintings. Eleni saw that Mr Papas looked a little sad.

'Perhaps next time I'll see a picture that I like,' Mr Vitalis said. 'Thank you for the coffee,' he said to Eleni.

'That's all right,' Eleni said.

After he left, Eleni went back to the kitchen. She began to wash the coffee cups. Then she looked out of the window at the café. The waiter was standing outside now. Mr Holland was still sitting at his table, reading his book. Another person was sitting down at a table behind him.

It was Mr Vitalis.

Mr Vitalis called the waiter and spoke to him. The waiter brought him a glass of wine. Mr Vitalis read his newspaper.

Eleni went back into the shop. There were three tourists looking around. Eleni stood ready to help. Mr Papas was talking to a woman who seemed interested in a painting in the window.

A man brought a book to Eleni. 'I'll take this one, please,' he said.

11

Eleni took the money, and then the man and his wife left the shop.

She looked across at the café again. Mr Vitalis was paying the waiter. A few minutes later, he walked back to his car. He left his newspaper on the café table, Eleni noticed.

Soon, Mr Holland got up to leave. He turned and looked behind him. Then he picked up Mr Vitalis' newspaper and put it under his arm.

'Why can't he buy one?' Eleni thought.

◆

Mr Vitalis left the café and went back to his car. He drove past the shop belonging to Mr Papas and out of the town. Soon he was on the road to Eagle House. It was a steep, narrow road. The big car had to slow down to turn the corners. Other cars waited for Mr Vitalis to pass.

Mr Vitalis knew the road well. He didn't have to think about his driving. He was able to think about other things – to worry about his computer company.

'There's not much more time,' he thought. 'I have to have money soon. Something will have to happen quickly if I'm going to save my business. It's been a bad year. Business has been poor. I've lost money in other ways, too. I've had to sell other businesses which I owned on the island.'

He did this secretly. He didn't want other people to know about his problems.

He looked up at the big white house, standing high on the cliff top. 'Perhaps I'll have to sell Eagle House, too,' he thought. 'If that happens, I'll have to leave the island. I can't live here in a small house. People will laugh and say, "Look at him now! He's not a big, important man now!" I don't want that.'

Mr Vitalis was afraid. As a young man, he knew how to be poor. But not now. It was easy to forget.

'I've made a lot of money in my life,' he thought. 'Some honestly, some not.'

Mr Vitalis didn't worry about this. When he had to cheat someone, he didn't think twice about it.

His wife cheated him a long time ago. She took his money and went away with another man. Others cheated Mr Vitalis when he was younger. But nobody cheated him today. He was too clever for that.

Now he was in trouble. Money trouble.

But Mr Vitalis had a plan.

He thought about the man in the café. 'Will he do what I want him to do?' Mr Vitalis thought. 'If he doesn't, I'm in trouble. There's no time to find another man. There's no time to make another plan. He *has* to do it.'

He arrived at Eagle House and pushed a switch inside the car. The tall metal gates opened slowly, and he drove through them. The gates closed and locked themselves after him.

Chapter 4   The Real 'Mr Holland'

That afternoon, Costas went to the beach and looked again at Eagle's Rock. He sat in the sun for an hour and looked up at the bird-shaped cliff. Eleni thought it was ugly. But Costas thought it looked beautiful. He imagined himself climbing the Rock. He imagined the feeling.

'I'm going to be famous!' he thought. 'Everyone on the island will hear about the climb. All over Greece, people will talk about Costas Kazakou, the famous climber! Even my father will know that I'm brave and clever. I *must* get to the top!'

Costas thought he knew the best way to the top now.

'I'll make the climb soon,' he decided. 'It's stupid to wait. I'm ready. I'll choose a fine, clear morning.'

Later, he was smiling to himself as he walked home. He went past his father's holiday villa. Suddenly, he saw the man Holland at one of the windows. Mr Holland was looking through binoculars at something.

Then Costas saw that he was looking at Eagle's Rock.

Costas crossed the road. He stood where Mr Holland couldn't see him. He watched the man. Mr Holland looked at the Rock for a long time. Then he moved the binoculars up, and looked at Eagle House. At last he moved away from the window.

Costas started walking again. 'I don't understand,' he thought. 'What's Mr Holland doing? Why is he so interested in Mr Vitalis' house? And why was he looking at Eagle's Rock? Is he going to try to climb it, too?'

Costas stopped suddenly. His eyes became wide with surprise.

'Now I remember!' he said. 'Now I know where I've seen Mr Holland's face before!'

After supper, Costas took Eleni into his bedroom.

'What is it?' she asked. 'You were very quiet during supper.'

'I know where I've seen Mr Holland before,' he said.

'You do?' Eleni said. 'Where?'

'I'll show you.' Costas went across to some bookshelves under the window. He took a book from the top shelf and gave it to her.

Eleni looked at it. It was a book about mountain climbing; *High Adventures*, by David Ashken. 'What's so special about this book?' Eleni said. Costas had many books about climbing, and a lot of them were by David Ashken.

Costas took it from her and turned it over. On the back was a picture of the writer of the book. He had a beard, but Eleni knew his face.

'It's Mr Holland!' Eleni said. 'So this is the kind of book that he writes.'

'Not now,' Costas said.

'What do you mean?' Eleni asked.

'Mr Holland's real name is David Ashken,' Costas said. 'He was a famous climber.'

'Was?' Eleni said.

'Yes. He had a bad fall from a mountain in Austria five years ago,' Costas told her. 'Another man was climbing with him. The other man was killed. After that, Ashken was too frightened to climb again.'

'Oh,' Eleni said. 'But why does he call himself Holland?'

'He's afraid!' Costas said. 'He doesn't want people to know him now. He was famous when he was a climber. Now he's nobody.'

'Why do you sound so angry about it?'

'I thought he was one of the best rock climbers in the world,' Costas said. 'I wanted to be like him. I read all the books about his climbs. But then he had the accident and became frightened. He became a coward. I don't like cowards.'

15

'He says he's a writer,' Eleni said.

'His books were about climbing,' Costas said. 'Now he's too frightened to climb. What can he write about? Nothing. He *says* he's a writer. But he doesn't write.'

'Poor man,' Eleni said. She felt sorry for Mr Holland.

'Don't say anything to Father,' Costas told her. 'He mustn't know who Mr Holland really is. He'll ask Ashken to try to stop me climbing. He'll try to frighten me. He'll tell me I'll probably be like Ashken in a few years. But I won't be. One day I'll be a great climber.'

'Like David Ashken,' Eleni said quietly. 'Right?'

Her brother didn't answer. After a minute, he said, 'Listen. Ashken was looking at Eagle House through a pair of binoculars earlier.' And he told her about 'Mr Holland' at the villa window.

'What's the problem?' Eleni said.

'Just think for a minute,' Costas said. 'Mr Vitalis has a house full of paintings. Many of them are worth thousands of pounds.'

'I know,' Eleni said.

'Ashken isn't famous now,' Costas said, 'so he needs money. Perhaps he's heard about Mr Vitalis' paintings and is planning to steal them.'

'That's a silly idea,' Eleni said.

'Mr Vitalis often talks about his paintings,' Costas said. 'Even to strangers. Perhaps Ashken knows about them.'

'It still doesn't mean that he's going to rob Mr Vitalis,' Eleni said. 'Eagle House is safe. Only a person inside the house can open the metal gates. And if anyone climbs over the fence, the police will know. Everybody on the island knows that. Nobody can get in and take any of Mr Vitalis' paintings. The only way is up Eagle's Rock, and that isn't possible–' She stopped suddenly.

'David Ashken was able to do it five years ago, before the accident,' her brother said. 'And he was looking at it through the binoculars this afternoon.'

Eleni looked surprised. 'But he's too frightened to climb since his accident. You said so.'

'I know,' Costas said. He became angry. 'But perhaps Ashken *will* try to climb the Rock, because he wants to get into Eagle House. Eagle's Rock is *my* climb. It's my way to become famous. Ashken isn't going to climb Eagle's Rock first!'

He wasn't worried about an old man and his paintings. He was only worried about David Ashken climbing Eagle's Rock.

'Ashken can't tell anybody if he climbs the Rock,' Eleni said. 'Not if he steals Mr Vitalis' paintings too.'

'But people will know if paintings disappear,' Costas said. 'It's the only way that a thief can get into Eagle House. He mustn't do it first. Eagle's Rock is mine. *I* must be first!'

'You can't! You'll kill yourself!' Eleni said. 'Promise me that you won't try, Costas.'

Costas said nothing.

Chapter 5   Mr Vitalis' Plan

David Ashken sat next to the window of the villa. He was looking through his binoculars. He could see Eagle House across the C-shaped beach, on the other cliff top. He could see the high electric fence on three sides of the garden. He could see the tall metal gates that opened on to the cliff road. Gates that were only opened by a switch inside the house.

'Mr Vitalis knows how to keep people out,' Ashken thought. 'There's only one way into Eagle House, and that's from the cliff side. Up Eagle's Rock. He was right. But can I do it? Can I make the climb?'

David Ashken's first meeting with Mr Vitalis was in England, a month earlier . . .

♦

Ashken was working in the bar of the hotel where Mr Vitalis was staying. Mr Vitalis saw him and knew his face.

'You were a climber, weren't you?' Mr Vitalis said.

'That's right,' Ashken said. 'But please don't say anything to other people in the hotel. I've told nobody here. They haven't guessed who I am. Only you know I was a famous climber.'

'So why are you working in a bar?' Mr Vitalis asked.

'Because I need money,' David Ashken told him. 'I needed a job.'

'I see,' Mr Vitalis said. And he watched Ashken thoughtfully for the rest of the evening.

The next night, he spoke to David Ashken again.

'I need money, too,' Mr Vitalis said. 'Perhaps I can help you – and you can help me.'

Ashken was surprised. 'How?' he asked.

'Do you think you can make one more climb?' Mr Vitalis asked.

Ashken began to shake. 'No,' he said. 'No, I don't.'

'Not even if you're paid a lot of money?' Mr Vitalis said. 'Then you can stop working in bars.'

'Why do you want to pay me a lot of money for a climb?' Ashken wanted to know.

And then Mr Vitalis told Ashken about the paintings in Eagle House.

'Some of them are worth many thousands of pounds,' Mr Vitalis said. 'I want somebody to steal them, and then hide them for two or three weeks. And then I want them back again.'

David Ashken began to understand.

'And you'll get money from the insurance company,' he said slowly. 'Then you'll sell the paintings and get money for them twice. Very clever. You'll sell them to somebody who has other stolen paintings. Somebody who'll keep his mouth shut. I've heard that there are people like that.' He smiled. 'Who is it?'

'You don't need to know,' Mr Vitalis said. 'You'll get the paintings out of the house. Then you'll hide them until I want them. You don't need to know what happens after that.'

David Ashken looked at Mr Vitalis for a long time. Then he said, 'Tell me about the house. What's so special about it? Why do you need somebody who can climb?'

So Mr Vitalis told him about Eagle House and Eagle's Rock. 'It must look real, when you rob the place,' he said. 'And nobody can get in over the fence or through the metal gates because of the burglar alarm. The police will be able to catch the robber before he can escape. The only way in is up the cliff.'

'So you need somebody who can climb Eagle's Rock. Somebody who can get into the house that way,' said Ashken. 'And somebody who will keep quiet because they need money. Somebody like me.'

19

Mr Vitalis smiled. 'Yes,' he said.

Ashken thought for a minute. 'How will I get out of the house with the paintings?' he asked.

'Through the metal gates to the road,' Mr Vitalis said. 'You can switch off the alarm and open the gates from inside. Then you can leave that way with the paintings.'

Ashken looked thoughtful.

'Will you do it?' Mr Vitalis said. 'I'll pay you well.'

'I – I don't know,' David Ashken said. 'I'll tell you before you leave the hotel.'

Ashken didn't sleep well that night. He had bad dreams and woke up two or three times. But three days later, he spoke to Mr Vitalis again.

'I'll come to the island and look at Eagle's Rock,' he said. 'I can't promise anything until I've seen the climb.'

'All right,' Mr Vitalis said.

'And I shall want half the money when I arrive,' Ashken told him.

'Agreed,' Mr Vitalis said.

♦

That was a month ago . . .

Now, David Ashken sat in the holiday villa, looking at Eagle's Rock. It was between the white house and the beach.

'Steep and dangerous,' Ashken thought.

Money, that was the problem. He had to have money to buy a business. A shop, perhaps. The money from Mr Vitalis was enough for that. He couldn't write books since the accident. And he couldn't keep other jobs.

'I can't work for other people,' he thought. 'I know that now. I have to be the boss, but that takes money.'

Most of Ashken's money was gone now. The books stopped

selling after he stopped climbing. Nobody wanted to buy a book by a climber who didn't climb.

'I'll have to make this climb – one last climb,' he told himself. 'There's no other way. Then I'll have the money to buy a shop or a small company.'

Ashken's hands began to shake . . .

He looked back at Eagle's Rock.

'No,' he said after a minute. 'I – I can't do it.'

He picked up the phone.

'Vitalis?' he said, when somebody answered.

'Yes,' said the voice at the other end. 'Who's that?'

'It's David Ashken,' Ashken said.

'And?' Mr Vitalis said.

'I can't do it,' Ashken said.

Mr Vitalis became angry. 'But you must! You *have* to do the job! My company's lost money and I've lost money in other ways, too. I need a lot of money quickly. And I've paid you half, as I promised. I left it in the newspaper in the café and–'

'I'll send that money back to you,' Ashken said.

There was a silence at the other end. Then Mr Vitalis said, 'Listen, perhaps I can pay you more when I have the insurance money.'

'More money?' Ashken said.

'Yes,' Mr Vitalis said. 'I'll pay you another ten thousand pounds.'

'Another ten thousand!' thought Ashken. 'That will solve a lot of problems. Exactly how many thousands of pounds are his paintings worth?'

'So what are you going to do?' Mr Vitalis said.

'I – I don't know,' Ashken told him. 'Give me a few more days and I'll decide.'

'All right,' Mr Vitalis said. 'Two days, no more. I can't wait for longer than that.'

Ashken put down the phone. He looked back at Eagle's Rock. Another ten thousand pounds!

Was he able to do it?

Chapter 6   The Climb

Eleni woke up suddenly. What was that noise? Was it somebody opening and closing the door of the house? But who was leaving the house at this time of the morning?

She looked at the clock next to her bed. It was 7 a.m.

Eleni got out of bed and went over to the window. She looked out. It was a bright, sunny morning. She could see the sea from her window. It was flat and blue. She decided to go for a swim.

She looked down into the garden below – and saw Costas!

He was carrying his climbing helmet and wearing his climbing boots. And he was walking quickly away from the house. Eleni knew immediately what her brother was doing. She knew why he was leaving the house so early.

He planned to climb Eagle's Rock!

Eleni opened the window to shout after him. Then she stopped herself. She didn't want to wake her father and mother. She didn't want her father to be angry with Costas.

'What can I do?' she thought. 'Can I stop him before he begins to climb?'

She quickly put on some clothes and opened her bedroom door. The house was silent. Eleni went downstairs, making as little noise as possible. Then she hurried out of the house.

Eleni ran down the hill to the cliff road. She couldn't see Costas anywhere. She ran past her father's holiday villa and down the steps to the beach.

It was empty except for her and her brother. She could see him now. He was almost at the bottom of Eagle's Rock.

'Costas!' she called.

But he didn't hear her. He was putting on his climbing helmet, looking up the cliff.

'Costas!' she shouted again.

This time he did hear. He turned round quickly. He looked angry to see her.

'Go back home, Eleni,' he shouted.

He found places for his feet at the bottom of the cliff. Then he began to climb.

'Costas, please come down!' Eleni called after him. 'It's too dangerous to climb alone!'

'Don't worry,' he shouted. 'I'm all right.'

He didn't answer her after that. Eleni watched him make his way up the cliff. She was frightened, but she couldn't stop him. She shook – not with cold, but with fear.

Up and up he went. Quite quickly at first, then more slowly and carefully. His body was flat against the rock. He tested a hand-hold, a foot-hold. He climbed up a crack in the rock. His feet were against one side of the crack, and his hands held onto the other side.

Eleni watched, her mouth dry.

'I can't shout after him again,' she thought. 'He won't stop now. I'll just have to hope that he'll be all right.'

Small stones fell from above as a bird flew off a shelf. The stones from the shelf hit Costas' helmet and then fell down to the beach. The bird flew away. Costas just continued climbing, slowly and carefully.

Now he was getting nearer to the overhang – that part of the Rock which was shaped like the beak of a bird. It was the most dangerous part of the climb. From there, the other three climbers fell and died.

Eleni watched, her hands half-covering her face.

Costas moved more slowly now. He stopped three or four times with his face against the rock.

'He's frightened,' Eleni thought. 'Oh no, he's really frightened!'

'Costas!' she cried out.

Costas didn't move for a long time. The ugly, bird-shaped rock was above him. Then he put out a hand. He found a hold. He moved one of his feet . . . and slipped.

Eleni screamed as more small stones fell from the cliff.

Costas tried again, and again his foot slipped. Now Costas cried out too. But he held onto the rock. He didn't move.

'Costas!' Eleni shouted.

He didn't look down, but he shouted something back.

'I can't hear you!' Eleni shouted.

'I can't move!' Costas shouted again.

♦

David Ashken watched the boy on the rocks. He was looking through the binoculars. At first, he didn't believe what he was seeing. Somebody was climbing up to Eagle House!

'Has Mr Vitalis found another person to steal his paintings?' he thought.

And then Ashken understood. It was just somebody climbing the cliff.

'Somebody brave,' he thought. 'Or stupid.'

As he watched, he remembered things.

Things that he wanted to forget.

He remembered another rock, another cliff, in Austria. A cold winter's day...

There was another climber with him. Guy Landberg. A younger man who knew less about climbing than him. Landberg always wanted to climb with the great David Ashken. Again and again, he asked Ashken to take him on this climb. And, at last, Ashken agreed.

It was a terrible climb... the two of them, with the rope between them ... the cold black rock against Ashken's face... the wind cutting across them ... the fine snow in Ashken's nose and mouth in the seconds before they fell ...

And the sound of Landberg's scream as he fell. The wind took the sound and carried it away. But Ashken could still remember that scream ...

David Ashken broke both legs and a shoulder.

Landberg broke his neck and back. He died before help could get to them.

Accidents happen when you climb. That's what other people said. But a small voice inside Ashken repeated the same question: Did he do everything possible to keep them safe? Later, he lay in the hospital bed and hoped to die. He climbed that rock again and again in his dreams. He woke, shaking. His skin was wet with fear. The sound of Landberg's scream rang inside his head.

Ashken didn't climb after that. He was finished as a climber, he told himself.

But now?

Now he watched a boy on a cliff. A boy who had no fear of climbing. A boy who still had his nerve. David Ashken wanted to be like that.

But... there was something wrong! The boy wasn't moving. He seemed unable to continue.

And a girl was running across the beach.

'She's coming here!' David Ashken thought. 'There's something wrong and she's coming here!'

Chapter 7   The Call for Help

Eleni ran back across the beach. She couldn't run fast on the soft sand. It seemed to take a lifetime to reach the steps on the other side.

'I have to get help,' she thought, as she began to climb the steps. 'Oh, poor Costas! Father will be so angry with him for climbing Eagle's Rock.'

Eleni ran up the last few steps to the cliff top. She had to find a telephone. Where was the nearest phone?

Then she remembered. The nearest one was in her father's holiday villa. She ran towards it.

She knocked loudly on the door. 'Mr Ashken! Mr Ashken!' she shouted. 'Come quickly!'

There were sounds from inside the villa, and then David Ashken opened the door. He looked at Eleni in surprise.

'What – what did you call me?' he said. 'My name's Holland.'

'You're David Ashken, the climber,' Eleni said. 'But that doesn't matter now. Can I use your telephone to call for help? My brother's on Eagle's Rock. He's too frightened to move.'

'Come in,' he said, looking worried. 'The phone's in the sitting room.'

Eleni ran across the room and picked up the telephone. Then she stopped. She turned and looked at David Ashken.

'Wait a minute!' she said. 'I don't need to phone for help. *You* can help my brother. You're a famous climber. You've climbed mountains. You'll know what to do.'

Ashken's face went white. His hands began to shake. 'I don't know. I–'

27

'Please!' Eleni said. 'Oh, please!' She took Ashken's arm, and pulled him towards the door.

'No!' Ashken said, pulling back. 'I can't do it!'

'Yes, you can!' Eleni said, angrily. 'Aren't you planning to climb Eagle's Rock and get into Eagle House?'

Ashken looked at her. 'How – how do you know that?' he asked.

'Costas saw you looking at Eagle House and Eagle's Rock through your binoculars,' Eleni explained. 'We guessed what you were planning. Somebody's paying you to steal Mr Vitalis' paintings. We're right, aren't we?'

David Ashken didn't speak for a minute. Then he said, 'You can't prove that. Nobody will believe it if you tell them.'

'I can tell Mr Vitalis what you're going to do,' Eleni said. 'He'll believe it. And I *will*, if you don't help my brother!'

Then Ashken laughed. 'So you'll tell Mr Vitalis? That's a joke.'

'I don't understand,' Eleni said.

'Mr Vitalis paid me to come to the island,' Ashken said. 'He wants me to steal some of his paintings.' Suddenly, David Ashken didn't worry who knew this. 'But I'm not going to do it,' he continued. 'So I'm not going to climb Eagle's Rock.'

Eleni was nearly in tears . . . 'But you must help my brother! Perhaps he'll die!' she said. 'Do you know something? Costas thought that you were the greatest climber in the world. He's read every book that you've ever written. He once dreamed of being like you. Now he thinks you're a coward. Show him he's wrong, Mr Ashken. Show him you're not afraid. Help him now. Please!'

Ashken looked at her for a full minute without speaking. It was the longest minute of Eleni's life. Then he said in a quiet voice, 'I don't think I can.'

'You can!' Eleni told him. 'Oh, I'm sure you can. You *must*!'

'All right,' Ashken said after a minute. 'But I – I have to get some things.' And he went into the next room.

Eleni looked out of the window as Ashken got his climbing things. The binoculars were on the table in the middle of the room. She picked them up and put them to her eyes. Then she looked across at Eagle's Rock. She could see Costas. He was still in the same place.

'He hasn't fallen,' she thought thankfully.

'Let's go,' David Ashken said from behind her.

She put down the binoculars and followed him out of the villa.

◆

A few minutes later, they were hurrying across the beach.

'I'm glad you came to the island,' Eleni said. 'But I don't

understand. Why does Mr Vitalis want somebody to steal his paintings?'

'For the insurance money,' Ashken said. 'Mr Vitalis isn't as rich as he wants people to believe. His company's losing money.'

Eleni looked surprised. 'Is that true?' she said.

'It's true,' Ashken told her.

'How did he find you?' Eleni asked as they half-walked, half-ran across the sand.

'I met him in England earlier this year,' David Ashken said. 'I was working in the bar of a hotel where he was staying. He knew my face. Then he learned that I needed money. He needed money, too. He wanted me to make just one more climb.'

'But what about the paintings?' Eleni asked. 'What did you plan to do with them?'

'Vitalis told me to keep them for a few weeks and then give them back to him,' Ashken said. 'He planned to sell them to a man with a private gallery. This man doesn't worry about where his paintings come from. Vitalis needed somebody who could climb. And somebody who needed money.'

'And he found you,' Eleni said.

'Yes,' Ashken said.

'Did you plan to hurt him? He probably wanted it to look real for the police,' Eleni asked.

'Yes, he told me to do that,' Ashken agreed.

They were almost at the cliff now. They could both see Costas. He was still in the same place. Eleni and Ashken didn't speak again. They began running faster towards the cliff.

David Ashken looked up at the boy on Eagle's Rock. Ashken was wearing climbing boots and carrying some rope. He looked for a way up the rocks. It wasn't easy. Maybe up that crack. And then across to the shelf to the left of the boy, he thought. Yes, that looked possible . . .

The ugly bird-shape of the rock hung over Costas. Then Ashken

it seemed a long, long way away. But now was the time. Suddenly, he knew that he had to make the climb. He had to save that boy.

'Hold on!' David Ashken shouted to Costas. 'I'm coming up to you!'

Chapter 8   Climbing Again!

Ashken began to climb. Slowly, very slowly, at first. He was shaking. His hands couldn't hold the rocks because they were shaking too much. He was afraid, and he knew it.

He closed his eyes as he remembered his accident on the Austrian mountain.

. . . He was falling, falling. . . There was snow everywhere . . . it was in his mouth, in his nose . . . He could hear the sound of his leg breaking . . . but he felt no pain at first . . . the cold froze the pain until later. . . He could hear himself scream . . . but worse than that, he could hear Landberg's scream . . . The sound seemed to fill his head . . . It seemed endless . . .

'Mr Ashken, hurry, please!' Eleni's voice came from below him.

Ashken opened his eyes. He wasn't on the Austrian mountain. He was still on Eagle's Rock. The boy was still above him.

'I can't,' he wanted to say. But he couldn't get the words out of his mouth.

He moved a hand, a foot. He was climbing!

He moved across the face of the rock. He worked his hands nd feet into cracks and pushed his way up . . . up . . . up. His arms med to know what to do. It was a strange feeling.

ee the shelf now. He could also see the boy's face as looked very frightened.

'Help!' Costas called out. 'Please, Mr Ashken, help me!'

David Ashken looked down at Eleni. She wasn't looking now. Her hands were over her face.

He looked back at Costas. The boy couldn't stay there much longer.

David Ashken climbed up. The sun was getting higher in the sky. He was hot. The sea was like a flat, blue mirror behind him.

His hands weren't shaking now. His feet found foot-holds more easily. Up and up he went. The shelf got nearer and nearer. The ugly head of the 'eagle' came between him and the sun. He could feel a soft wind on his face. He couldn't hear the sound of the sea. He thought only about his feet and his hands. The climb was the only thing in his mind.

He was climbing!

He couldn't believe it. After five years, he was really climbing again! All his old skills returned. He began to feel that he was part of the cliff, like before the accident.

'Have I really been away?' he thought.

At last, he got to the shelf.

'Costas!' he shouted across to the boy. 'Are you all right?'

'I – I'm frightened,' Costas shouted back.

'Don't worry,' Ashken told him 'I'll get you down. You'll be safe now. Listen. You're going to come over to me–'

'I can't,' Costas shouted. 'I can't move!'

'Yes, you can,' Ashken said. His voice was calm. 'You will do exactly what I tell you. Do you hear me? Just listen to me.'

'But–' Costas began.

'There's a foot-hold to your left,' Ashken continued. 'Can you see it? It's half a metre away. Find it.'

'I can't–'

'Find it!' Ashken shouted.

After a minute, the boy moved his left foot and found the foot-hold.

'Good,' Ashken said. 'Now move your hands. Move carefully, and you'll be all right.'

The boy moved his hands. Suddenly, he was less afraid. David Ashken was up here with him. 'Everything will be all right,' Costas thought. 'I'll get down. This man knows what he's doing.'

Slowly, step by step, Ashken guided Costas across to the shelf. He told him where to put his hands and feet. One move, one hold at a time.

On the beach below, Eleni took her hands from her face. She wasn't afraid to watch now. Ashken was telling Costas what to do.

Costas moved closer and closer to David Ashken. Then they were together, and David Ashken put the rope around the boy.

'You can get down to the beach now,' Ashken said.

Costas said, 'All right.' He was calmer now. He didn't look afraid. 'Thanks.'

Ashken smiled. 'It's OK,' he said.

He held the rope as Costas went down the face of the rock. Then the climber went down after him.

Ashken's fears were gone.

'I've never felt better in all of my life than I do now!' he thought, as he went down the cliff face.

When they were both on the beach, David Ashken looked up at Eagle's Rock. He knew that he wasn't afraid to climb again. But more important than that, he knew that this was his last climb on Eagle's Rock.

'I'm not going to take Mr Vitalis' paintings,' he thought. 'I'm a climber again! I'm not a thief. I'll never be a thief. I'll earn my money honestly. I'll climb other rocks and mountains. I'll write more books. I'll become famous again.'

He looked at Eleni and Costas.

Eleni smiled. 'Oh, thank you, Mr Ashken!' she said. She threw her arms around him.

'Yes,' Costas said. He was shaking. 'Thank you again.'

'No, I must thank you,' David Ashken told them. 'You helped me to climb again. You've changed my life. Do you know that? I'm not afraid now.'

Costas looked back up the Rock. 'I think I'll stay away from this part of the cliff,' he said.

David Ashken smiled. 'That's a good idea. Eagle's Rock is too dangerous. It's probably even too dangerous for me. But that doesn't matter. There are plenty of other places to climb. And good climbers don't go into unnecessary danger.'

They walked back across the beach.

'Will you climb with me again while you're staying on the island?' Costas asked him.

'Yes, I will,' David Ashken said. 'We'll climb together.'

Costas looked pleased. 'That will be great,' he said.

'But first I have to telephone someone,' Ashken said. 'He's hoping that I'm going to do a job for him.'

Eleni looked at him. 'You mean Mr Vitalis?' she said.

Her brother looked surprised, but he said nothing.

'That's right,' Ashken said. 'But I'm not going to do that job. I don't need to do it now, because I can climb again.'

'I'm glad,' Eleni said.

'I am, too,' David Ashken said. And he walked off across the beach.

'I didn't know he knew Mr Vitalis,' Costas said to his sister. 'What's it all about?'

Eleni smiled. 'I'll tell you as we walk home,' she said.

And she did.

ACTIVITIES

Chapters 1–2

Before you read

1 Look at the Word List at the back of the book.
   a What are the words in your language?
   b Which of the words are used to talk about:
      • rocks and climbing?
      • crime and money?
      • birds?
      • buildings?

2 Read the Introduction to the book and then answer these questions.
   a The action in this story happens on an island. Where is the island?
   b What does Costas want to climb, and why?
   c How does his sister feel about that?
   d What kind of story will this be? Will it be funny, sad, exciting or frightening?

While you read

3 Write short answers to these questions.
   a What time of the year is it? ....
   b Who is nervous? ....
   c Whose villa is he going to? ....
   d Has he been to the island before? ....
   e Who is Costas's father? ....
   f What does Costas enjoy doing? ....
   g What is the name of the house on Eagle's Rock? ....
   h How many people have climbed to the top of Eagle's Rock? ....
   i Who goes to the holiday villas with Costas? ....
   j Whose face does Costas already know? ....

After you read

4 Who says or thinks these words?
   a 'I don't have to do it. There's still time to say no.'
   b 'Half the money now. The other half after the job's done.'
   c 'He's a better climber than he was.'
   d 'I don't want burglars. So I tell everybody about my burglar alarm.'
   e 'I want to be the first person to climb it to the top.'
   f 'He's staying at the villa for two weeks. He's a writer.'
   g 'Mr Holland seems nervous.'
   h 'Where have I seen Mr Holland before?'

5 Work with another student and have this conversation.
   Student A: You are Mr Kazakou. You don't like Costas climbing rocks and cliffs. Explain why.
   Student B: You are Costas. Explain why you love climbing. Try to change your father's mind about climbing.

Chapters 3–4

Before you read

6 What do you think will happen next?
   a Will Costas climb and fall from Eagle's Rock?
   b Will a burglar try to get into Eagle House?
   c Will Mr Holland go back to England?
   d Will Costas remember where he saw Mr Holland before?
   e Will we find out who is employing Mr Holland?
   f Will Eleni try to climb Eagle's Rock?

While you read

7 Are these sentences right (✓) or wrong (✗)?
   a Eleni works in Mr Papas's shop in the school holidays.   .....
   b There are a lot of tourists in the shop that morning.   .....
   c Mr Vitalis never buys paintings from the shop.   .....
   d Mr Holland picks up Mr Vitalis's newspaper.   .....
   e Mr Vitalis is working for Mr Holland.   .....
   f Costas sees Mr Holland looking at Eagle's Rock.   .....

g Mr Holland was a famous climber. .....

h Costas is worried about Mr Vitalis's paintings. .....

After you read

8 In which order do these happen?

Number these sentences 1–5.

a Eleni sees Mr Holland in the cafe. .....

b Mr Papas takes Mr Vitalis into his gallery. .....

c Mr Vitalis has a drink in the cafe. .....

d Mr Vitalis arrives home at Eagle House. .....

e Mr Holland picks up Mr Vitalis's newspaper. .....

Now number these sentences 1–5.

f He shows Eleni a book. .....

g Costas decides to climb Eagle's Rock soon. .....

h They think that David Ashken is going to steal
some paintings. .....

i He realises that Mr Holland is really David Ashken. .....

j He tells Eleni Mr Ashken's story. .....

9 Explain what Mr Vitalis's plan is. Why has he made it? Why has he chosen David Ashken to help him?

Chapters 5–6

Before you read

10 Discuss these questions. What do you think?

a Where did Mr Vitalis first meet David Ashken?

b What was Mr Ashken doing at that time?

c What did Mr Vitalis ask him to do?

d Why did Mr Ashken agree?

While you read

11 Write one word in each space.

David Ashken was working in a hotel .... when he met Mr Vitalis. Mr Vitalis knew that he was a famous .... Mr Ashken and Mr Vitalis both needed ...., so Mr Vitalis asked for Mr Ashken's help. He wanted Mr Ashken to steal and then .... his paintings. Mr Vitalis will get money from his .... company. Later, he will also .... the paintings. The only way into the house for a burglar is up the ....

In London, David Ashken agreed to .... at Eagle's Rock and think about the job. But he is .... of climbing, and now he doesn't want to do it.

Eleni wakes up at .... o'clock and sees Costas in the .... He is wearing his climbing .... She .... him to Eagle's Rock, but he starts .... At the dangerous overhang, Costas's foot .... He can't ....

David Ashken watches and remembers the .... of another young climber. Then he realises that something is .... with Costas, too.

After you read

12 Work with another student and have this conversation.

  Student A: You are a reporter and you work for a television company. David Ashken is in hospital after his accident. It is big news. Ask him questions about the accident and about Guy Landberg.

  Student B: You are David Ashken. Answer the reporter's questions. Explain how you feel about Guy Landberg's death and about climbing.

13 Describe a time when you lost your nerve. What happened next?

Chapters 7–8

Before you read

14 Discuss how these people are going to feel at the end of the story, and why.

  a David Ashken
  b Costas
  c Mr Vitalis
  d Eleni
  e Mr Kazakou

15 Use one of these words in each question. Then answer the questions.

How Who Why What

a .... doesn't Eleni telephone for help?

....

b .... knows that he has to save Costas?

....

c .... does David Ashken put around Costas after he reaches him?

....

d .... does David Ashken feel about climbing on the way down?

....

e .... does he decide to earn money in future?

....

f .... don't good climbers do?

....

After you read

16 Why does the story end well for:

  a Eleni?

  b Costas?

  c David Ashken?

  d the insurance company?

17 Why does the story end badly for:

  a Mr Vitalis?

  b Mr Kazakou?

18 At the end of the story, David Ashken says that he has to telephone Mr Vitalis. Act out the conversation with another student.

19 Work with another student. How many famous climbers do you know? Choose one and find out more about them. Are they alive or dead? Why did they start climbing? Where did they climb? Why did they become famous? Why did they stop climbing?

Writing

20 You are on holiday on the island. You see the boy on Eagle's Rock. You also see the man helping him. Write a postcard to a friend at home. Describe what happened.

21 You are Eleni. David Ashken is back in England. Write a letter to him and thank him for his help. Tell him how you feel about his past, and his future.

22 You are Mr Vitalis. You still need money, so now you need another plan. What will it be? Who can help you? Write about your new plan in your notebook.

23 A very rich person has offered you a lot of money if you do something dangerous. What is it? Will you do it? Write him or her a letter. Give your answer and explain your feelings.

24 Write about a time when you, or someone in your family, was in danger.

25 Choose a picture in the book and write about it. What can you see in the picture? Who can you see? What are they doing? What is going to happen next?

26 You work for a travel company. You think that climbers will enjoy trips to the island. Prepare a page for the Internet, telling people about the place and about your company.

27 Write about this book for your school magazine. Is it a good story? Will everybody enjoy it? Why (not)?

Answers for the Activities in this book are available from the Pearson English Readers website. A free Activity Worksheet is also available from the website. Activity worksheets are part of the Pearson English Readers Teacher Support Programme, which also includes Progress tests and Graded Reader Guidelines. For more information, please visit: www.pearsonenglishreaders.com

WORD LIST

alarm (n) a loud noise that tells you about danger. People have alarms on their cars, for example.

beak (n) the hard, pointed mouth of a bird

binoculars (n pl) a pair of glasses that you hold in front of your eyes. They show you things that are a long way away.

burglar (n) someone who steals things from buildings. Burglars go into a building from outside.

cheat (v) to be dishonest in the way that you get something

cliff (n) a high, steep rock along the coast

coward (n) someone who is not brave enough

crack (n) a long, narrow space in something where it has broken

eagle (n) a big wild bird that eats small animals

edge (n) the place where something stops

fence (n) something that goes around a piece of land. Fences are made of wood.

gallery (n) a room or building where you can look at pieces of art

helmet (n) a hard hat that protects your head

insurance (n) an agreement that a company will pay the costs of an accident or problems with travel, for example. You pay money every week, month or year for the insurance.

nerve (n) the ability to stay calm when you are doing something dangerous

overhang (n) a piece of rock that hangs out above air

rope (n) something strong and thick that you tie things with

slip (v) to move across the floor in a way that you cannot stop. You can slip on a hard, wet floor, for example.

villa (n) a house with a garden in the country or near the sea, often a house used for holidays

worth (adj) the amount that something can be sold for